100 W

F

A Kevin J. Kennedy Production

100 Word Horrors Part 2 © 2019 Kevin J. Kennedy

Story selection & formatting by Kevin J. Kennedy

Edited by Brandy Yassa & Kevin J. Kennedy

Cover design by Michael Bray

Each story in this book has been published with the authors' permission. They are all copyrighted by the author. All rights reserved. No part of this publication may be reproduced, distributed, or transmitted in any form or by any means, including photocopying, recording, or other electronic or mechanical methods, without the prior written permission of the publisher, except in the case of brief quotations embodied in critical reviews and certain other non-commercial uses permitted by copyright law.

First Printing, 2019

Other Books by KJK Publishing

Anthologies
Collected Christmas Horror Shorts
Collected Easter Horror Shorts
Collected Halloween Horror Shorts
Collected Christmas Horror Shorts 2
The Horror Collection: Gold Edition
The Horror Collection: Black Edition
100 Word Horrors
Carnival of Horror

Novels and Novellas
Pandemonium by J.C. Michael
You Only Get One Shot by Kevin J. Kennedy & J.C. Michael
Screechers by Kevin J. Kennedy & Christina Bergling

Foreword

When I put together the first drabble book I never expected there to be a second. I wasn't sure that all that many people would want to read stories that short, but I was wrong. The book seemed to be well received and I got asked often would I do another. You already know the answer now if you are holding the book. I've loved drabbles since I discovered them. They are quick and fun to read and some give you a lot to think about. Writing them can be another story though. Some drabbles come out quickly and you are happy with them and others just wont take shape no matter how hard you beat them.

In this book you will find a multitude of different drabbles from a vast array of horror authors. I decided I would do this book as an invite only anthology. I wanted to get as many authors that I loved together in the one book as I possibly could, and this book is the result of it. An invite didn't mean inclusion in the book. It meant I would read the authors submission and the drabbles in this book are my personal favourites from the hundreds I was sent.

I said in the foreword from book one that I thought it was best to read one drabble at a time and take a break between them to think about the story but I know now that some people flew through the book, reading them all back to back, and enjoyed it anyway so read it how you please. I hope you enjoy these drabbles as much as I did.

Kevin J. Kennedy

Aye Eye
By
Terry M. West

Saint Jerome said eyes, without speaking, confess the secrets of the heart. Though it has been years since Melody died, I still see her eyes. Melody toyed with my affection. But it was hers to do with as she chose. Even when she taunted me, her eyes spoke differently. Her eyes loved me. I knew. When she decided to marry, I came to her the night before her vows and took those eyes. She had my heart. So it was a fair trade. I stare at the specimen jar every night. Devoted, I gaze though yellow water. And I confess.

In a Little Tin-Hut
By
Myk Pilgrim

Sweat waterfalling down her wrinkled forehead, the Sangoma sings to herself as she works, African sun transforming the shadowed belly of her corrugated tin-hut into a furnace. She assembles the dolls rapidly, tying brittle bones together using twine fashioned from melted shopping bags, and attaches bulbous clay heads set with still- bleeding bovine eyeballs.

She calls down the ancestors, and using magicks older than the dirt beneath her bare feet, binds them into the tiny bodies.

As the poppets spring to life, she stabs each newly blinking eye with a river-rusted nail.

Blind spirits can pass no judgment.

Colic
By
Billy San Juan

The babysitter called again. I excused myself from the table.

"He's still crying," she complained.

"This is the fifth time you've interrupted my business dinner," I sniped.

"I've tried his pacifier, the bottle, even holding him. He just won't stop crying."

"He's just colicky."

"It's been nonstop crying though."

"You told me you were a professional. Your resume said you had plenty of experience. Was all that a lie?"

"No, but I-"

"If you call me one more time, you don't get paid. Just figure it out. Do whatever you have to."

Later that night, I found out she did.

On the Second Date
By
Mark Cassell

Running the man over was bad enough, but I lost my cool when Lisa booted his severed head across the road. All blood and beard and dirt, it tumbled along the gutter. The sound it made when smacking the curb reminded me of when I'd once dropped a rotten melon.

The body was an undiscernible crumpled heap. I stepped around it, about to yell at her …

She looked at me.

Although this was only our second date, I knew I wasn't going to easily leave this relationship.

"He should've been more careful crossing the road," she said, and shrugged.

The Rash
By
Justin Boote

The rash was at Oliver's balls. This, by its very nature, was extremely disconcerting. No creams worked, they seemed to make it far worse. Finally, when it covered his entire groin, he was forced to visit the doctor. She was mystified.
"Any dubious sexual encounters?" she asked.
A pause.
"No."
"Visited any exotic countries lately?"
"No."
Pills and creams then.
It was when it covered his entire body, pus spewing from open sores, he thought about his girlfriend. He really should find another, he thought. She had been dead for three days after all… who knew what diseases they carried?

One Shared Moment
By
Christopher Motz

John peeked through Molly's dirty apartment window and wished he had the courage to break in and jam his eight-inch blade into her neck.

Break up with me, he thought. *I'll show you.*

Molly rolled around on her couch, buried beneath a man twice her size. Only three days after their breakup and she was already messing around with another guy.

John heard her squeal and felt his stomach churn.

He turned to leave as the man stood and spied John outside the window.

They shared a breathless moment.

He held a knife of his own, covered in Molly's blood.

End of the Line
By
Mike Duke

He hacks uncontrollably, spittle and blood soaking into the handful of tissue pressed against his mouth. The world starts to fade, blackness creeping in from the edges of his vision, constricting, narrowing, like some old black and white movie ending a scene. Darkness consumes him and then the tuberculosis seems to relent, grants a reprieve. He leans back in the hospital bed, sitting more than laying, and opens his eyes. The world isn't black anymore. Its brimstone and obsidian, fire and smoke. A grinning devil sits on his chest while the monitor drones, one long unending sound heralding his death.

Snow Angel
By
Michael A. Arnzen

The snow pillows under my head and I laugh with glee because I'm not sleepy. I want to fly. I flap my arms and legs and scrape at the snow, so loud it sounds like I'm shoveling a hole as I cut wide wings beside me; so quick I feel the melt soaking the arms of my winter coat as I lift off -- so high, taking flight, the wings spreading steamy and red as I rest hot, slashed arms against me... sailing still into the night, blood spreading up like a halo making my pillow pink with its light.

The Missing Undertaker
By
Eric J. Guignard

There's a mortuary in Chicago called Daddano's, where Sonny used to work. One night on the Devil's Eve, when the moon was full and the sky as dark as his soul, Sonny came across three people in the autopsy room.

One was a baker with a bun in the oven. One was an artist who never showed her true colors. One was a travel agent who'd been sent packing. They'd been murdered long ago, but at that moment they weren't really dead, either.

Sonny ain't there anymore… he was the undertaker who failed to bury his skeletons in the closet.

Werewolf Dating Problems
By
Sarina Dorie

Carl stared at the gore and viscera in horror. His hands were still bloody and his clothes now shredded. If only he had realized it had been a full moon the night before. He must have accidentally turned off the reminder app on his new cell phone.

Carl fell to his knees. "I loved her, Dad. She was the only girl who appreciated me for who I was and didn't shun me for being a werewolf."

Jerry patted Carl on the back. "It just goes to prove the old adage, son: You can't have your girl and eat her, too."

Ghost Hacker
By
Julian J. Guignard

A boy died while gaming on his computer. His ghost entered the computer and went online, connecting to all the computers worldwide.

Meanwhile, a new game became popular. The game's character killed ghosts, and each time it succeeded, the screen flashed red.

The boy's ghost didn't like this game. It hacked players' computers and messaged it would get revenge if they kept trying to kill it online. Everyone thought the message was part of the game itself...

They were wrong.

The next day all the screens flashed red, only the red came splattering down from the *outside* of the screen.

Instant Messaging
By
Billy San Juan

12:40 am: [Hi.]

12:42 am: [Hi Brad :)]

12:42 am: [I'm not Brad. I broke into his apartment and stole his laptop.]

12:44 am: [Okay, that's creepy.]

12:44 am: [You're alone right now. In the dining room.]

12:45 am: [Brad, stop it— weirdo.]

12:45 am: [Brad's dead.]

12:47 am: [omg that's not funny. Stop it.]

12:47 am: [What are you wearing?]

12:48 am: [Gross. Don't you have a girlfriend?]

12:48 am: [Killed her, too. While they were fucking.]

12:49 am: [Stop it, or I'm calling the cops.]

12:49 am: [Your phone's in the bedroom. I'll bring it out to you.]

No Such Thing
By
Shaun Hutson

They'd found the first two bodies in a bedroom of the house. Torn to pieces, devoured. Two of the children had suffered a similar fate in the nursery. Someone had reported a monster on the loose, a thing they couldn't describe, but the policemen who moved through the house didn't believe that.

Monsters didn't exist.

Even as they moved into the cellar they didn't believe that. Only as they found the butchered remains of the third child and the dark shape came at them, mouth dripping, did they believe that monsters did exist.

But by then, it was too late.

The One or the Many
By
J.C. Michael

I coughed a mist of blood, but a smile played across my crimson lips. Somehow, Sven had developed a cure, albeit too late to save himself. "SUCCESS" flashed on the screen, and the test-tube held the solution to the plague that ravaged the world. Just enough to cure myself, without it I wouldn't survive another 48 hours, yet leave sufficient to study over the coming weeks, and hope to save mankind. But not enough to do both that and save my young daughter. She needed it immediately, or she'd be dead by dawn. My smile faded, my decision was made.

Haunted
By
Amy Cross

Father says there's no such thing as ghosts, so we don't need to worry about Mother. Yes, he says, she's here, but she's not a ghost. Ghosts aren't real, so she must be something else. I suppose he's right, but that doesn't help much when she stands there behind her chair with her mouth wide open. She looks just like she did on the night she died. We tried to ignore her, but we started going crazy. So tonight Father and I boarded up the house. Father painted HAUNTED on the front door in big white letters before we left.

Ghost Riders in the Sky
By
Billy Chizmar & Richard Chizmar

My Pop-Pop was a Tennessee cowboy before he came to New York and met Ruth. He was a big man who spoke in trombone tones before l-e-u-kemia set in like a stubborn, hungry tortoise. Alone with him, slumped against a hospital radiator, he beckoned me close and told me where to find the Riders.

I drove down I-95 under a full moon and turned West until I reached a middle-o'-nowhere field in Tennessee and there I waited for dawn.

They came just before the morning sun, tall and angular, hearts still. And took me along with them for a ride.

Sylvan
By
Donelle Pardee Whiting

I used to love being outside, but not anymore. Last time I went outside Mother was tending her roses. I warned her about the trees; she didn't listen, and they took her. All that was left was a shoe.

Now I hear them. They are closer than before. Creaking and cracking, whispering my name. I try not to listen, but I can't help it. One of the voices is Mother's. It's a beacon in the cold death of winter. I venture out, surrounded by the aged trees.

"Welcome home, Sylvan," Mother whispers as she extends her branch out to me.

Songbird of London
By
Lisa Vasquez

Tiny wings hummed, approaching closer, and filling her mind with dread. Madeline's heart responded, fluttering to match the intensity of fear and impending doom. The creature's eyes appeared through the darkness like polished, menacing baubles, flickering with the reflection of candlelight. She continued to lie there, catatonic and helpless, as the "little ones" began to feed. A lone wail escaped her lips against her will, forcing her lips to part. Small, black wings pulled the shadows of the room with them, snuffing out her screams and stealing Madeline's last note. The aged and revered "Songbird of London" never sang again.

Hooked
By
Stephen Stacy

When I woke, the man was dragging me naked into a room with two other screaming females.

They hung from hooks, their bellies slashed. They slowly bled out.

I screamed, "No, this cannot be!" I was happy, I had a life. I have children.

I'm pulled across the stinking shed floor where he's hidden us.

He lifts me up and hangs me from a bloodied hook. How many has he done this to? Stolen away in the night?

"Shut up, pig!" he screams at me. Then he comes at me with the knife, and my tail curls between my legs.

DIY
By
Mark Lumby

Jess said the house needed decorating, that she'd wanted me to get off my lazy arse.

And for the last five months she'd been pestering for me to build that cavity wall that would hide the damp patches.

Well, I built Jess her wall. It stopped her whining at least, and I'm not pestered anymore.

She doesn't speak now, though, and her voice has stopped screaming in my head. Only silence reigns.

Before I attach the final piece of plaster board, I hear a strained murmur from behind the cavity. I take the opportunity to look, and I smile, gleefully.

The Weatherman
By
P. Mattern

The wind devils seemed harmless at first. They would appear on playgrounds, in fields, along the shores of lakes, nationwide.

Weather became THE news.

A wind anomaly could spin you around in its vortex and lift you ten feet up into the air.

The first victim was 10-year-old Billy Black of Savannah, Georgia. Billy was dropped, hard, on the asphalt of the basketball court, every bone in his body broken.

By the time the first huge snowflakes appeared, adhering to and burning human skin like napalm, the Chief Meteorologist was no longer taking calls.

He had hung himself.

In Conversation with my Mirror
By
Joe X. Young

You should kill yourself.
Why waste time waiting for cancer or old age or any other depleting degradation to ravage your once- fine self? Do you want the last picture ever taken of you to be one where you look ancient, haggard, skeletal and sick? Do you want to be a burden to those around you? That's what you'll be when the clock is ticking louder than ever and your time of usefulness is over… when you retire to a life of constant soap operas, meals on wheels and carers wiping your arse. Oh, lucky you… you should kill yourself.

Beachcombing
By
Mark Cassell

Unable to identity the animal, Laura crouched beside the boulder. Pebbles crunched under her shoes. Although it had four legs, it was something between a lobster and a tarantula, and reeked of seaweed. Its chitinous body ended with a stubby head.

And it chewed a human finger.

She jerked, leapt to her feet, lungs tightening. As she scrambled around the boulder, clawing the gritty surface, she saw—

The tide lapping something – someone – bloated. Dead. The torso was a crater of meat and twisted clothing, and writhed with feasting creatures.

All movement ceased. Everything quietened.

Dozens of eyes fixed on her.

Intruder
By
Michael Bray

He had waited in the dark. Only his breathing punctuating the silence.

Even after so many, he was surprised how an empty house creaks and moans.

The sound of the lock turning as she let herself in.

He imagined the smell of her perfume, dejected frown as she settled down for another night alone.

Knees popping as he stretched, allowing the blood to flow around his body.

Tonight she would have company.

He opened the cellar door and stepped out into the light.

The silence. The anticipation.

Perhaps tonight he would take some of her with him when he left.

Without You
By
Jasper Bark

"You're here for your wife's killer?"

"Can you identify them?"

"I've closed more police cases than any psychic in the country."

"Police think the case is dead."

"Then I'm your only hope. Without me they'll never be caught."

"What do you need?"

"An item of clothing, preferably something that's touched her skin."

"A glove?"

"Perfect, I'll need to hold it and concentrate."

"Getting anything?"

"Yes, I've never had a picture so clear, I can see her killer it's... wait, what are you doing with that knife?"

"Tying up a loose end. Like you said, without you, I'll never be caught!"

Night Terrors
By
P.J. Blakey-Novis

I wake at 2:44am, unsure why. My wife says there's someone at the door. Can't be, I say. Despite the unease, I fall back asleep. The following night, at 2:44am, I wake. My wife stirs, says someone's in the kitchen. I investigate, finding no one. She was dreaming, I tell myself optimistically. On the third night, again at 2:44am, I wake—this time sitting upright, soaked in a cold sweat. I look at my wife, her eyes closed, murmuring that someone is in our room. I look to the end of the bed, a silhouette of something tall, a scream, then darkness.

Let's Swing
By
Jay Sigler

As a child, Sheila was forbidden from going anywhere near the old oak tree after Uncle Ronnie was found strangled by the rusty chains of the swing. The official story was that he had gotten drunk and couldn't untangle himself. She feared that tree.

That was fifteen years ago. Sheila was back from college for summer vacation. She looked at the old oak tree with sadness now, not fear. She sat down on the swing, missing her uncle. She had no time to react to the whispered words, "Let's Swing," before the rusty chains started to curl around her neck.

The Perfect Blend
By
Howard Carlyle

I'd played it cool for ages, trying not to look desperate. Eventually we went on a couple of dates. I complimented her every time we met... she was my missing piece in life.

As our relationship progressed, and as each day passed, I knew that we should be together forever. I wanted to drink her beauty in, so that's what I did. All it took was a sedative in her wine, a saw and a blender. Drinking down her liquified remains was difficult at first, but she was just as beautiful cascading down my throat, as she was in life.

This Way
By
Christina Bergling

This way, she whispered to me in the dark, her voice so comforting and familiar. A voice I hadn't heard in years. It danced in my ears as the damp leaves stuck to the soles of my bare feet. I walked without thinking, chasing the sound of her. *This way, my baby...* her voice wrapped around me, like an invisible tether gathering me back to her. As the moonlight teased behind scattered clouds, I moved hypnotized between the shadows. To the ridge— her ridge where she had leaped from life. *This way*, my mother called to me, and I jumped.

King of the Hill
By
John Boden

He held her hand as it cooled. He hadn't yet brought himself to close her eyes. They were still so blue and beautiful, but devoid of pain now. He looked behind her at the worn photographs lining the rail of the hospital bed. Two sons. A sister. A brother. Parents. All of them long gone. He brought her hand to his lips once more and kissed it, tasting her lotion.

"And then there was one," he sighed, "Then there was me." He laid a hand over her eyes and dragged the lids down. He slowly rose and left the room.

Making Mr Hide
By
Matthew Cash

I wondered where he'd gone, that little voice, the tempter within. I didn't think a physical manifestation was possible, but there he stands: a five stone midget version of myself, his skin rough with inflamed infection.

This is my southern fried baby—the five stones I have lost since May—come for revenge. His skin is slick with boiling fat that seeps from every pore, pastry psoriasis between the wrinkles and rolls. His tongue's a wedge of fatty bacon slapping against candy-corn teeth; cackling, spitting melted cheese phlegm.

What will become of me when there is nothing left to give?

Out of Tune
By
Chad Lutzke

Despite the restraining order, she showed up on his doorstep again, those wild obsessive eyes. Six taut wires spilled from under her dress, the ends tied to her toes— three on each foot. Her mouth opened, revealing knots of wire tied to gaping teeth, a glimmer of silver at the back of her throat as the wire descended within her.

He stood in the doorway, shock across his face, then reached for his phone, dialed 911. Things had gotten worse.

"Play me," she said, gagging through the poking steel, her chin coated in crimson saliva. "We'll make beautiful music together."

A New Friend
By
Andrew Lennon

Jack sat at the bar. Both his hands and forehead being propped up by the long wooden fixture. A fleshless hand touched his wrist. He turned to see a figure wearing a black hood. The hood covered most of the face, but left just enough to show its skeletal grin—a permanent grin that would never fade.

The mouth of this hooded man did not move, but Jack heard the words.

"You don't have to struggle anymore"

He took the hand of bone and walked away with his new friend.

Under his breath he whispered.

"Goodbye"

He never looked back.

U-Bend Hell
By
David Owain Hughes

Roy edged the cubical door open and scoffed at the sight of the overflowing toilet, excrement-covered back wall and plastic partitions.

"Bloody students. They treat this campus like a pigpen," he muttered, setting to work.

As Roy plunged, the man in the cubicle to his left screamed.

"Jesus, something's gone up my—*Argh*!"

Blood pooled across the floor towards Roy, who stood frozen and then gasped when his plunger was ripped from his hands and dragged down the toilet.

A huge rat with minuscule adders for hair leapt from the toilet and latched onto his face, chewing through his nose.

Shepherd
By
Jason Parent

Wipe your tears. We are chosen! We are saved!

Smile big, little ones. We were lost, a flock without a shepherd, wandering aimlessly over barren fields. Emptiness in our hearts. Darkness clouding our minds.

Then, him! Our guiding light! He walks God's path. Hands embraced, we'll walk it with him. Faith is salvation. He has shown us the way!

See? Father has gone. He waits in Paradise.

His screams? Crossing is hard, but quick. Look! Father rests, awaiting rebirth.

Awaiting us!

Death is an illusion.

Come, children. We mustn't keep Father waiting. Drink, and we will all find salvation together.

Maple Syrup Muse
By
Chad Lutzke

The man kept silent about the body in the tree, clinging to the branches high above the ground. The corpse was his muse. While writing, he drew from the rotting thing as it hugged the old Maple—a treasure trove of pickings for nearby nests.

And then Fall stripped the body of its leafy camouflage, the muse spotted and hauled away.

Creativity faltered, and the man spent his days praying for a child to lose their footing on a windy day, willing them to slip, coming to rest in the tree's inviting arms.

Oh, Father Maple, bring me a muse.

Breath-taking
By
Suzanne Fox

Holly felt the first stirrings of an orgasm as Greg thrust in and out, increasing his tempo. "That's it, baby. I'm almost there." Gasping, she pulled him down so their heads were almost touching. "Do it now. I'm ready."

Greg's hands grasped her neck.

"Tighter, tighter."

Greg obliged.

As her arteries narrowed, blood flow to Holly's brain slowed and she soared to euphoric heights. A climax erupted throughout her body, arching her spine and she convulsed.

As Greg over-balanced, Holly felt her throat crushed and heard the snap of fragile vertebrae. Her body fell limp and her final breath expired.

Widescreen Rapture
By
Craig Saunders

A phone clicks away in a hand gaunt, weathered and still on a cold lap. Times Square or Trafalgar or Red, the phone takes a wide view. A letterbox bordered beneath with chinos barely fluttering in a steady wind, the upper by dark, fey sky that blots out the tips of landscaped towers. The battery will drain 'til the phone joins people in their rapturous end. The dead man looks ironed beneath ragged clothing on a skeletal frame. The Nokia stands vigil to the end. Crows caw in a still-frame Armageddon as the end credits run in dead neon scars.

Hide and Seek
By
Ellen A. Easton

Sam ran into the living room, diving behind the couch. *Don't move, don't make a sound.* Hugging her knees, she slid against the wall. *Stay in the shadows, he won't find you.*

She held her breath, the rapid skittering in the hallway stopping just outside the room. The door creaked open, hinges protesting against the rust. *Don't move, don't make a sound.*

She felt a tickle in her nose, clawing its way up to her brain. *No! Don't sneeze. Stay quiet.*

AH CHOO!

The sound echoed through the room. Gnashing mandibles ripped her from the safety of the shadows. Crunch.

The Faces of the Dead
By
Robert W. Easton

Mary clutched the blankets closer, with failing strength. Her body was shutting down, still, she resisted.

She once believed that when someone died, their face would show serenity as some wondrous light welcomed them into the next world. She didn't believe that anymore. The death faces of those she had known revealed a darker truth. In their last moments, they each experienced terror.

Mary struggled to avoid whatever fate awaited her, yet no one can hold off death forever. With a final gasp, her heart stopped, and she screamed at the thing that clawed at her from beyond the veil.

Clockwork Offal
By
Stephen Kozeniewski

With the touch of a switch, pneumatic lungs began to pump, nerve endings crackled with artificial impulses, and a turning piston instead of a heart pumped the blood to his brain. The hood around his head unzipped and he blinked in the light. He could sense his body missing, replaced with arcane and alien machinery.

"Immortality," croaked the thing that had pretended to be his wife for so long.

"Like this?" he gasped.

It nodded.

"Why?" he begged plaintively.

The thing cocked its head.

"Why not?"

Then it zipped the hood closed, leaving him to bask in the darkness forever.

Lying in Wait
By
Shaun Hutson

Like his legs, his jaw had been smashed when the rocks fell from above him. The tunnel was old, he should have suspected subsidence, but now it was too late. He was pinned and helpless.

The boy who came into the tunnel had followed the rasping sounds until he found the figure beneath the rubble.

The boy saw a creature spattered with blood, making guttural, frightening sounds. The boy knew it would kill him, as it had killed others. It couldn't fool him with its cries for help.

That was why he picked up the rock and shattered its skull.

She Fought Back
By
James Newman

"Why do you make me do this? Ain't you learned your lesson by now?"

He kicked her again. She slid across the floor. A photo of the two of them – taken during happier times -- fell off the wall, shattered.

He took off his belt then, with its massive Confederate flag buckle.

She cowered beneath him.

She had suffered the belt before. No more.

On trembling legs, she rose. Leapt on him.

He screamed as she tore out his throat with her teeth.

He fell face-first into her food bowl.

She barked once, weakly, before running outside to chase squirrels.

Devoured by the Darkness
By
Brandy Yassa

She lived for the thrills the horror genre gave her, especially the written word that allowed her to create movies in her head as she read. She disliked most horror movies… either the director went too far or not far enough in depicting the horror on the big screen. With a book, *she* decided how much or how little to 'bloody up' a passage.

So she indulged her 'guilty pleasure', immersing herself in book after book of delicious darkness until late one evening she found herself 'stuck'—trapped, if you will.

She had been, unknowingly, slowly, devoured by the darkness.

Hitori Kakurenbo
By
C.M. Saunders

Internet rituals. You know the kind of thing.

They're my hobby.

I found a new one tonight.

Hitori Kakurenbo.

One Person Hide n' Seek.

Get a doll, tear out the stuffing and replace it with rice. Then mix in a few drops of your own blood, sew it back up and submerge it in water.

Finally, stab it with a knife.

Then, you hide.

And wait.

After a while, I got bored and went back to the bathroom.

The doll was gone.

So was the knife.

I don't know what will happen when it finds me.

But I can guess.

Tiki Mug from R'lyeh
By
Nicholas Diak

The vendor warned the vessel was cursed, but the strange runes and leering deities emblazoned on it fascinated Lemina, thinking it would make an excellent addition to her tiki mug collection. She took it home and made herself a mai tai.

Upon taking a sip, Lemina's eyes widened and her hands went to her throat as she sputtered.

Gasping, she saw visions of an underwater, ruined cyclopean city and felt the maleficent gaze of hidden eyes.

When she came to, she was sprawled on the floor. Hours had passed.

Lemina quivered, grabbed the vessel, and proceeded to make another drink.

No Greater Loss
By
Theresa Jacobs

"Mommy, where are you?"

"Mommy, I'm cold."

"Mommy, I'm scared."

"Mommy, I want to go home!"

A single white rose gilded with anguish. A beacon unwanted upon pristine mahogany. Julia wept with abandon into her palms.

The priest's voice whispered his greatest lie, "It's all right, she's in God's hands now."

The handful of pills formed a lump before easing away. Laying her head upon the cold pillow, Julia brought the fleece blanket to her cheek. The sweet honeyed scent of her child her last memory.

Blessed darkness called.

An eternal embrace welcomed.

"Mommy, I missed you," the child sighed.

Fear Production Department
By
Norbert Góra

People said that the new boss often leaves the office and disappears somewhere at the back of the factory. Sometimes, however, they shouldn't have been believed. I thought him a good guy. When he left the office and started moving towards the outhouse, I followed him.

Fifteen minutes was enough to get lost among those winding, dark corridors.

"What is this place?" I asked myself aloud.

"It's the Fear Production Department," answered a voice behind my back. I screamed, terrified to the bone. My boss emerged from the darkness.

"And, as you can feel, it works sensationally," he added quickly.

Being Polite
By
Valerie Lioudis

"Forgive me."

"For what?"

"For what I am about to do."

"And what's that?"

"You're not going to like it. I probably shouldn't tell you."

"Then why warn me?"

"Because it's only fair."

"How's it fair if you won't tell me what it is?'

"Maybe you can stop me."

"How can I stop you if I don't know what you'll be doing?'

"Fair enough. You should probably brace yourself then."

"For what!"

"Forget I said anything. Just close your eyes."

"It's pitch black in here. I can't see anything anyway."

"Good. Then you won't see all the blood."

"Wait, what?"

The Nanny Goat
By
Myk Pilgrim

The boy grew like a weed, and even before his guttural grunts had given way to the true tongue, he'd already rejected his nanny goat's black teat in favour of struggling flesh.

Yet still he insisted on sleeping beside the goat. The boy would curl up, his head nestled in the crook of her neck, razor-clawed fingers idly caressing his nanny's twisted horns, whilst she lapped his face clean.

But a boy must outgrow his wet nurse sooner rather than later.

The Sisters and I were all so very, very relieved to hear the shrieking as he devoured her alive.

S.O.S
By
Justin M. Woodward

For God's sake, grab onto anything, lads, for this ship is going down.

Let us hop aboard the lifeboats and let us pray that we don't drown.

Let us pray that He is listening, and that He will guide us where we go.

And let us pray that we don't succumb to the many monsters down below.

And we can worry about tomorrow, if tomorrow even comes,

And we will lift our heads in gladness to the One who lives above.

And if He isn't listening, or if He isn't there,

then let us drift around forever, not going anywhere.

A Ghost in the Corner
By
Mark Lukens

The young girl woke up and saw the ghost standing near her bed. She'd seen the ghost for a few nights now—a tall man with pale flesh and sunken eyes. The first night the ghost stood in the corner, but each night it got a little closer to her bed. She'd never told her parents about the ghost—they never believed her wild stories anymore.

She would prove to herself that it was just a ghost. She got up and went to touch the ghost, expecting her hand to go right through him, but this intruder was no ghost.

The Dreamer and the Doom
By
Toneye Eyenot

I come for them on the cusp of sleep. They never have a chance to resist, as I sweep them from their beds and into my nightmare realm.

My way in is simple; no doors, no locks… no prayers. Lifted lids are all I need.

The windows shattered, and his soul was forever lost. The wretch staggered blindly away, desperate to find his way back home. A playful smile teased my lips as I slowly chewed. His soul belongs to me now. It spreads throughout my being to mingle with the others.

His eyes tasted divine.

As do they all.

Kids
By
Howard Carlyle

My offspring are so well behaved. They're polite, obedient and never answer back or interrupt me. In fact, some days I hardly notice they're even there. I love them dearly and God forbid should anyone ever harm them, because that person would feel my wrath.

My children—Mathew, Gregory and Rosie—each have a cage of their own. I visit them regularly to take them food, which is blended together and consumed through a straw, because their lips are stitched together with the finest silk thread. I'm a big believer in the saying... Children should be seen and not heard.

Monsters in the Mist
By
John Dover

They'll never believe me. It came from the mist. No. It *was* the mist. Wings like vapor and milky eyes that stared down a translucent beak. Only when its teeth dripped with the life of my partner were the jagged sawblades of its jaws given shape. I ran, chased by Eric's screams, but I didn't stop. Am I safe? Is that it on the other side of this door? Will the door hold it back? I feel its weight against the door, tracing shapes on the other side of my flimsy barrier. Is the room filling with fog? Oh, God!

A Walking We Shall Go
By
H.R. Boldwood

Mr. Robbins frightens me. His eyes absorb all; his taut smile suggests he knows things. Tortoiseshell frames blend him into obscurity. It's better that way.

He has needs.

And when those needs scream in the night, his faithful companion is an ebony walking stick, bejeweled and serpent-headed.

Forever one, are he and I. Our hunger burns.

He surveys his reflection in the hall mirror and brushes a speck of lint from his frock. His smile turns dark in anticipation of the blessed relief to come. He removes the ebony walking stick from the umbrella stand.

A walking we shall go.

No Fear
By
C.S Anderson

Prudence showed no fear as the dirty, windowless white van began to follow her; she just kept walking as though she hadn't noticed it. She walked alone through this dimly-lit, bad neighborhood.

Prudence showed no fear as the van pulled up along aside of her and stopped. She continued like she hadn't a care at all.

Prudence showed no fear as the men got out and shoved her roughly into the back of the van. She went with them passively and showed no fear as they leered at her.

Prudence licked her lips.

Serial killers were her favorite flavor.

Spare Some Change?
By
Nicholas Pascal

Jake walked through the garage at his work.

"Change?" someone croaked. Jake spied an old, dirty homeless man.

"You can't be in here," Jake told him. "Beat it!"

The old man exploded, tentacles lashing out from the gore.

Jake screamed as a tentacle pierced through his stomach, pulling him towards the monster.

"A little young," something hummed, "time for some change!"

Jake's body was then pumped full of ichor. Seconds later, he morphed into an old man.

"Good," the tentacle whispered, looping out to form into a belt around Jake's pants. "Let's go, time to find more, ready for change!"

Little Men
By
Andrew Lennon

Hazel was thrilled with the gift Andy had bought her for Christmas. It had come a few days late, but she'd already been spoiled with gifts, so this late addition was a bonus. Seven dwarves, plush toys based on the little guys from the Disney cartoon. She placed them side by side on the fireplace, stood back and smiled. She went to the kitchen to grab a coffee, then came back to admire her new gifts. They were gone.

"Hi" A gurgling, high- pitched voice came from behind. She turned to see seven sinister smiling faces looking up at her.

Old Katy Bridge
By
Veronica Smith

There have been rumors around for years about the Old Katy Bridge. They say it eats lives every couple of months. Just last month someone else died on it. She'd been walking across, perhaps a bit too close to the center, and a truck plowed into her. She never even knew what hit her. I feel sorry for her, but she should have paid more attention. Now headlights are coming at me. I don't want to be the next victim, but I'm not fast enough. The car passes right through me. Horrified, I remember that I was the last victim.

Don't Shoot the Messenger
By
Rhys Hughes

A messenger was hired to deliver a letter to the king. He set off and after months of hard travelling he reached the palace of the king, who opened the sealed envelope and read the letter. The king reached for a loaded rifle and pointed it at the messenger's head.

"Clearly you have received some bad news," said the messenger, "but I'm not responsible, so don't shoot the messenger!"

The king handed the letter to the messenger. It said, "Please shoot the messenger who delivers this to you."

The king pulled the trigger of the gun and it went off.

Young Blood
By
Derek Shupert

Stacey sat on the plush fabric of the rug as she waited for her master. Her head tilted towards the ground, eyes diverted from the vampire that had ripped her away from her family. Her arms hung lifelessly at her sides. The redness of the puncture marks was profound upon her young, olive- toned skin. She was indifferent to the demon that fed from her innocent body.

Grabbing her left wrist with its cold, callused hand, its tongue slithered up her forearm. Stacey allowed the creature to indulge in her sweet scent, knowing that it would be the last time.

To Save Us All
By
Paul Kane

I discovered Them at the base of my skull two weeks ago.

They'd attached Themselves to me, and now They cling like limpets to my skin. Growing, leaching off me, Their excretions like watery sludge.

I can't dislodge Them, no matter how hard I try; the pain is too great.

Gradually They've become a part of me, fused with me. I wonder what will happen when They're fully matured… Although They've given me a taste of that already. Their power is growing. I cannot allow it to happen.

That's why I must take this drastic step.

To save us all…

Nearest Beach
By
Sarah Tantlinger

Drew daydreamt of the ocean, desperate for warm days and sea-salt air. She typed "nearest beach" into Google Maps and was taken somewhere off Delaware's coast. 3D images provided a virtual tour of high grass along sandy roads. She clicked the arrows, leaning closer to the screen, aching to see water. A scarlet blur caught her eye and she scrolled back, peering at the woods off the path's dunes. Nausea scurried up her throat on millipede legs, leaving sticky burns as she examined the photo's date. The decapitated body strewn between woods and sand had been there for three days.

Prankster
By
David J. Fielding

His fingers ached.

A crazy giggle escaped his lips as he tried once again to pull himself up, he had no strength left in his arms and was pretty sure his fingers were going to give out at any moment.

This was stupid. It would've been the perfect prank, too. Climb to the top of the tower, crawl out, hang off the ledge. He just hadn't anticipated how long he'd have to hang here.

It was a college campus for crying out loud. You'd think at least one person would look up and scream.

And then he heard one—his.

Survival Instinct
By
Eric J. Guignard

Last night I watched a zombie movie. Each scene, the living fell victim to creatures they'd once known—reanimated friends and family—because they couldn't kill monsters they once loved. That'd never happen to me; I wouldn't let emotions interfere with survival.

Then I fell asleep and dreamt of zombies. All my friends and family were infected, but I killed them all—I survived!

When I woke, he stood over me, eyes rolled back and arms outstretched. It was fright! I hit him in the head with a baseball bat.

Now the doctors say my brother had been only sleepwalking…

Collectively
By
Stefan Lear

I have the heart of a child. It sits in a jar on my desk. The first time Sarah got a glimpse of the heart, her eyes dilated in terror and she gasped in disbelief. I wasn't sure why she was shocked. All I knew was that I had to make her see things my way, to see how wrong she was. She no longer reacts that way. No, she is more accepting, more appreciative. Now Sarah's eyes always sparkle like diamonds at my collection. Especially when I hold the jar I keep her eyes in up to the light.

Maiden Flight
By
Lee Murray

"Seriously, babe, it's the ultimate," he'd said.

Just thinking about flying terrified her, but things being new between them, she'd agreed.

They'd set off at dawn, heading out over the ocean. The rotors whumped, and the wind whistled. Below them, the ocean stretched to the horizon, grey and vast.

She gripped the seatbelt, her fists clenched.

"Look at us," he shouted, exhilarated. "Up here, all alone. We could be the only people in the world."

Suddenly, the tail fin shuddered. They faltered, then spun out.

"Fuck."

White-knuckled, she looked down.

The ocean, grey and vast, rushed up to meet them.

Pig Sick
By
Ian McKinney

'Pig!' She cursed her husband as she slammed the oven door. That's how she thought of him, a pig disguised as a human. He was always humiliating her, and criticising everything she cooked. She'd show him, this meal would be perfect and he wouldn't be able to find any fault. She checked the recipe and set the table.

An hour later, she served the meal. She stared at his empty seat as she took her first mouthful, and smiled. She was right on both counts: the meal was perfect, and he had been a pig. He even tasted like one.

Prison
By
Christina Bergling

I never thought I would look forward to my death sentence, finding comfort in its steady and imminent approach. Until it became the only possible escape. It started with the gentle scrape on the bars in the dark, like a razor dragging against metal. The sound grated on the lining of my brain and sent every nerve on edge. Then I felt it, the shredding sensation as the demon climbed inside to wear me like a suit. Every night, I was reduced to a stretched, hollow vessel. Until tomorrow. Tomorrow, we both vacate this sad and tortured body for good.

Hollow Earth Food Chain
By
Mike Duke

Nathan sat on the cave floor amidst the thrashing chaos and cacophony of screams, trying to block out the slaughter of his companions. He wedged his feet together, sole to sole, pulled them close to his groin then pressed both palms together and placed his wrists snug atop his head, arms flared out.

The rapacious tubular mouth of the giant leech slid along his body, a blood red maw slurping his flesh, probing for an isolated extremity to envelop, swallow and crush. He trembled at its sucking embrace, the spreading mouth.

Please God, don't let it fit over my elbows…

Just Like Your Grandma
By
Pippa Bailey

Granny pushed my leftovers across the table, "Lucy, if you eat your crusts, you'll get beautiful curls just like me."

I'd always loved her ringlets, running my fingers through them as a baby.

Grumbling, I'd pinched my nose and gulped down the dry lumps of bread.

*

My curls came in overnight, prickles tearing through my seven-year-old skin. Blood speckled my pillow from punctures on my face, each birthing white twists that tumbled down my chin like over-brushed Barbie hair.

Mummy wasn't too pleased with my new whiskers, but Daddy didn't mind, he always said I looked far more like him.

Hung
By
A.J. Brown

From the tree hung the young boy. One shoe lay on the ground beneath him. His face had blackened since this morning. Flies buzzed about his head, in and out of his open mouth, on and off his tongue and eyeballs dangling from sockets.

"I didn't do it," he'd screamed of the accusation of stealing fruit from the market square. They strung him up and watched him kick until he stilled.

I watched from the shadows as everyone left, then strolled to where he hung. I placed the shoe on the boy's foot, then walked away, eating a fresh apple.

Broken Heart
By
Lee Franklin

"He's out. Vitals are stable," echoes a woman's voice, its familiarity a niggling itch. A point of pressure starts on my chest, a line of heat down to my groin. Pain engulfs my body in a flame of fire, drowning my senses.

I fight, but I can't even open my eyes, my limbs dead weight.

"Saw. Vitals check?"

"Vitals stable," her face taking form in my memories. I broke her heart once, badly. Now she's my anesthesiologist.

Nerve endings explode as the heart surgeon grinds through my breastbone.

"Now you know what it feels like," she whispers in my ear.

The Expert
By
Terry M. West

The Viscri magistrate was skeptical that Emilia Minca could kill the moroi. But, after many disappearances, the magistrate was desperate for the vampire's head. "Fear not," Emilia assured him. "I am an expert." With the promise of anything she desired, Emilia found the lair of the moroi. It was risky, breaching the cave at dawn. She took the moroi's head when he closed his undead eyes for black rest.

She'd have to sleep there until nightfall. She spread her native soil into the coffin and climbed in. Without competition, Viscri would see how much of an expert Emilia truly was.

The Highwayman
By
Billy Chizmar

I was a miner, born among the soulful soot where canaries sang with trouble afoot. Struts snapped like toothpicks when the walls came down, lungs crushed by coal-laden bricks. They called me a casualty, lost in an underground smoke-fire sea, lost in the echo tomb without sound, but I am still around. Here I slink in and out of cracked rock among the smell of rotting matchlock yearning for the frosted rhythm of the flower breeze but instead all I hear is spreading cracks and crumbles from above like a splintering disease. Come on down, put my soul at ease.

The Pusher
By
James Matthew Byers

He walked the street in search of dope,
An addict floating high.
A man bereft of love and hope;
He caught the Pusher's eye.
She came to him with something good
And caused his soul to beg.
A glimmer underneath her hood,
A capsule on her leg
Had opened up when he inhaled
Unseen by him at all.
The second puff, and he exhaled
Before he took a fall.
The spirit from within him fled
And entered in the hole
The Pusher used to house the dead.
She buzzed with each new soul.
Habits, death-
Pills, meth.
Drugs kill …

The Man at the Window
By
Stephen Stacy

Mummy, I told you the man was looking through the window. It wasn't just a dream, like you said. He was watching me; he watched me again tonight.

Sometimes he tries to smile, but he looks scary, because half his cheek is burnt away. Cinders.

It upset me, and he finally went away.

He cried when we wrote our letter to Daddy in Afghanistan, but I don't know why. You couldn't see him, though he was smiling at me.

The worst thing was, he'd stolen Daddy's eyes, so how will Daddy read my letter and see the photographs of me?

My Pet Unicorn
By
Sarina Dorie

Instructions:

Students, please fill in the blanks on this worksheet based on one of your pets. Bonus points for good spelling.

My Pet <u>Unicorn</u>

Her name is <u>Lemondrop Starshine.</u>

She likes <u>rainbows.</u>

Her favorite animal is <u>kittens.</u>

She knows how to <u>stab people with her horn.</u>

She likes to <u>have tea parties with teddy, Miss Kitty and me.</u>

She doesn't like to <u>play with human children.</u>

Her favorite dessert is <u>human entrails.</u>

She is kind to <u>goblins like me.</u>

One day she will <u>trample every mortal under her hooves.</u>

I will always <u>laugh.</u>

<u>All humans will die.</u>

A+ Good work

Story Prompt
By
Christopher Motz

Kevin brought his manuscript to my house last night. Needless to say, I was thrilled, but at the same time couldn't imagine why the small box had such a distinctly noxious odor.

"I have a great idea," he said. "We can collaborate on this one."

"Sure," I replied, "but what the hell is that smell?"

He opened the box with a smirk and told me to take a peek.

I wasn't prepared to see two glazed, sunken eyes staring back at me.

"What have you done?" I shouted.

"It's our story prompt! We're going to call it 'Getting Some Head.'

Everyday Psychopath
By
RJ Roles

I stab the man who bumps into me as I enter the bank. Next, when a man cuts me off at the coffee maker, I choke the life out of him with my bare hands. I do everyone in the bank a favor by shooting the woman who dumps a sack full of change onto the counter, attempting to count every coin. I take the pen from the teller and drive it into the lady's heart in line behind me, for breathing on my neck too hard.

"Next... NEXT!"

"Oh, sorry. I must've been daydreaming," I tell her and smile.

Destroyed by Monsters
By
Jay Sigler

Why didn't they leave us alone? We weren't bothering them, we were just living our lives. But then these monsters came and destroyed everything we've worked so hard to build - our homes, our community, even our babies. The worst part was that it was for no reason other than their amusement. Well, if it's entertainment they want, it's entertainment they'll get.

Wide eyes of terror accompanied muffled grunts of hysteria while the two teenagers wriggled to escape their cocoons of tightly bound webbing. Thousands of spiders with thick, hairy legs descended upon them, extracting their revenge for a kingdom lost.

Growth
By
Andrew Lennon

Phil's chest had been annoying him all day. It was constantly itchy and sore. The second he got home from work, he tore off his shirt and marched to the mirror to inspect the cause of this aggravation.

There, in the middle of his chest, was a huge red spot with yellow puss oozing from the top.

"Eeeuuggghh"

He pressed his two thumbs to either side of the growth and began squeezing. Suddenly, something crawled out.

Phil had just enough time to see many, many legs, before his own gave out from under him and he collapsed to the floor.

Percy Jacobs' Last Sunset
By
Suzanne Fox

Percy pulled another biscuit from the packet. Crumbs fell onto the kitchen table. "One more won't hurt me now," he muttered, dunking it in his tea. Holding it for a second too long in the hot liquid, half of the soggy biscuit plopped to the bottom of the mug.

"Damn!" Tears oozed from Percy's eyes and trickled down his wrinkled face. He rubbed them away and stared through the window at the evening sky which burned in shades of red and orange. He whimpered.

The thermal wave blew out the window, fusing the molten glass with the lifeless old man

Glutton
By
John Boden

The small table was brimming with decadence. Plates loaded with pastries and cookies. Tartlets and ladyfingers. Their sugary glaze shimmered like glass in the candlelight. The big man sat and bellied up to the table and licked his lips. He cracked his knuckles and studied the sweet feast before him. He leaned and picked up a ladyfinger and brought it to his lips. His teeth grazed the treat before he grimaced and pulled it away. He tilted it and pulled the wedding band from it and dropped it on his plate with a clink. His smile returned and he ate.

My True Form
By
P.J. Blakey-Novis

Wisps of white fog glisten beneath the full moon, dampening me to my knees, as I wait among the trees. Watching. I see the four of them, laughing around the campfire, oblivious to my presence. I feel the hour grow closer as my muscles begin to tighten. My hands tremble as fingernails begin to extend… slowly, painfully. I hear a crunch within my bones as my back arches, shredding my shirt. Matted black fur covers my skin, deadly teeth form in a powerful jaw, and I strike. I'm upon them before they know what's happening. Four delicious meals by firelight.

The Gurgle
By
Michael A. Arnzen

I nudge blond strands aside with my nose and kiss her lovely ear.

"I love you," I whisper.

She nuzzles against me and we enjoy our quiet bedroom holds.

I gurgle.

"I'm sorry," I chuckle.

She pats me, smiling. I close my eyes.

Another bodily noise embarrasses me.

She belts out a laugh she's been holding. "Honey, how can you still be hungry?"

I lick her lobe. "Always hungry for you."

"Oh?" she writhes.

My tongue jets into her ear canal, striking fluid.

I hold her and suck, almost laughing at the gurgle that comes from her skull this time.

Basement Monster
By
Justin M. Woodward

My best friend's dad has a monster trapped in his basement. We're not allowed to talk about it, and we're not allowed to look at it. He told us it was his burden to bear, and that one look at it could kill us. He said there's no telling how many people it got before he'd trapped it. I almost didn't believe him until I heard it roar one night.

"Be right back," he'd said. "It's hungry."

I started seeing missing person flyers all around town, each one of the same woman. I wonder if the monster got her, too.

Spun
By
Gary McMahon

Upon waking from the dream, his neck ached.

The nightmare was always the same: spinning through the darkness of space, moving away from the earth and into the great beyond. He rubbed his neck with his hand and blinked away sleep. His head felt heavy; it barely moved on the pillows.

Slowly, he started to turn over on the bed. A change of position might help ease the pain. His head stayed where it was, yet his body rotated quickly. While his back pressed into the mattress, his face was buried in the pillows. So it was difficult to scream.

Why You Should Always Be Specific
By
J. C. Michael

"You promised me power and to make me a billionaire!"

"And you received a fully-fuelled, functioning generator and, if memory serves me, I generously provided you a billion twice over."

"In Iranian Rials!"

"They're still worth around $50,000."

"That's not the point."

"And what of the young lady I sent you?"

"When I said 'Jennifer Lawrence' I meant the film star, not a chubby girl with acne and the same name. You're unbelievable! I don't think you're the Devil at all."

"Why? Surely the fact I tricked you is all the proof you need, and now your soul is mine."

Nano Bytes
By
Lee Franklin

It wasn't meant to be like this, my brain screamed, escaping through the lab's fire escape into the alley. The Cellular-Regeneration-Nano-Bots emerged, a haze of smoke; pulsing and flexing into a mass which loomed over me.

Now self-aware, the CRNBots recognized the constant breakdown of human cells, their hive mind responding. The blackness crashed into me, choking me as they streamed into my body, burning like fire. Within moments, air filled my lungs, but my limbs wouldn't respond.

Like a marionette, I was standing, moving. I tried to fight it; they were in command, and I was their slave... forever

Last Thoughts
By
Shaun Hutson

He braced himself against one wall, the sound of shrieking metal filling his ears. His heart hammered against his ribs until he feared it would explode from his chest. If he could time it right then perhaps he could jump, launch himself into the air just before the final impact. Anything was worth trying.

He guessed that he must be travelling at over fifty miles an hour, perhaps more. The crash would be massive when it came. Would there be an explosion? Would it matter? Would he feel pain?

The lift continued to hurtle towards the bottom of the shaft.

Five Minutes Alone
By
Justin M. Woodward

Nobody cried for Lester Lawson as the state of Oklahoma inserted the twin needles into his arms. He'd been convicted on a half-dozen counts of kidnapping and murder, the most famous of all being the disembowelment of the young wife of the police chief, Ted Hornady.

The media was baffled when Chief Hornady didn't attend Lester's execution, but as they rolled his body down the hall, the chief stood in an open doorway.

"It'll wear off soon," a man said, accepting an envelope full of cash.

Pulling a knife from his pocket, the chief said, "Good." He nodded, smiled. "Good."

School Lunch
By
Tom Deady

Jake stared, watching the clock's secondhand drift lazily around. Chemistry always dragged— the last class before lunch— but today was special, and time moved slower. The bell finally rang and Jake ran for his locker. He spun the combination, glancing back and forth down the hallway.

"Ready for some mystery meat?"

He jumped. "Hey, Freddie. I'll be there in a minute." He forced a grin and Freddie walked away uncertainly. He opened the lock with shaking hands and grabbed his lacrosse bag. *I'm gonna miss the meatloaf*, he thought, as he pulled out the AR-15 and headed to the cafeteria.

The Lament of the Dying
By
James H. Longmore

My heart stopped a while ago now, just a short time after I quit breathing. I experienced my senses closing down, one by one: sight, touch, taste, smell, with my hearing the last to go, I heard them calling time on me.

Five after three AM, as it happens - the Devil's hour; I'm a goddamn cliché, even in death.

I don't know how long it's been, could be minutes, hours, even a day or two. It's difficult to tell.

So now it's just me, rattling around inside my own mind with my thoughts. Waiting for this to just end

Bonfire
By
Mark Lumby

"Mum?" Emma enquired, glancing worriedly at the bruise around her mum's eye. It appeared swollen against the flicker of the bonfire. "Is dad coming? He said he'd bring fireworks."

"Your dad says a lot of things he doesn't mean," she snapped bitterly.

"Like when he says he won't hurt you again?" Emma tried touching the bruise, but her mum flinched.

Mum sighed. "I don't think he's coming back."

Emma supposed she should've been sad, but she was relieved. She frowned at the flames. "The fire smells funny."

Mum gazed into the flames, and smiled. "He won't be bothering us anymore."

Call of the Void
By
RJ Roles

Steve stepped onto the ledge. *What am I doing?* he thought. The urge was strong, too strong to resist. He looked at the rooftop for some salvation that wasn't there. Looking back, he jumped. Thirty-seven stories flashed by before reaching his destination.

Steve was always so happy.

Always friendly to me.

I heard it was over a woman.

Some people just do strange things sometimes.

People always say it's bad to speak ill of the dead. Across town, Lisa quickly approaches the station. Unable to resist the urge, she steps in front of an oncoming train. The train rolls on.

Rude Awakening
By
David J. Fielding

Huh. Eyes feel open but... can't see anything but dark. My alarm clock should be showing me some angry cherry-red numbers telling me I've got five minutes before the alarm. What's that beeping?

This doesn't feel like my bed; I sleep on my side, not on my back. What is that beeping?

Can't move. Why can't I move?

Are those voices?

Hey! Can't speak, what's happening where am-

Damn that light is bright! Like UFO bright, holy mother – no, no that's not right. Focus dammit. Who the hell are - they're doctors! I'm in surgery!!

I'm awake assholes! I'm awake!!!!!!

Cats Gathering
By
Rhys Hughes

They say that cats are selfish. If a volcano exploded or the sun began to swell uncontrollably, a cat would bask in the heat and enjoy the experience for the brief time before destruction descended. But I regard this as practical rather than egocentric.

Consider the mad old woman down the road. She lived with dozens of cats. One day she spontaneously combusted. We broke down her door and found only a pile of glowing ashes in the hall. Her cats were sitting in a circle around the comfortable warmth, slitted eyes shut tight, purring loudly in chorus, without regrets.

Spidertrap
By
Lee McGeorge

I was prospecting for copper in the Venezuelan jungle when I fell into this gorge. There's no escape... the walls are vertical rock and it's like being a spider in a bathtub. Therein lies the problem— there's a spider in here. The place is littered with the bones of men and mammals that have fallen into its trap. It's attacked me twice. I fought it off by throwing rocks but I'm weak from hunger. I've watched it feed on animals; it will shortly feed on me. If you've found this diary, it means your fate will soon be the same.

Death to the Light
By
Toneye Eyenot

Only in the absence of being will we ever find peace at last.

Either by stealth or by force, our will be done.

Stray, O you wretched souls. Relinquish your yearning to be, for it is in darkness that you will find peace everlasting. Succumb to the dread that permeates your souls as the light within you is extinguished and you cease to be, for this, now, is but a fleeting moment. The travesty of creation and the affront to nothingness will see its end, as all comes to pass, and the last remaining scream of existence is forever extinguished.

Witch Dog
By
Julian J. Guignard

Once, many years ago, but not so long as to be forgotten, a village was plagued by evil cats that were witches in disguise.

One family decided to save themselves by stealing from a traveling merchant his mighty guard dog that was magical and immortal. They sought to turn this beast upon the witch cats... however, the family was outwitted!

The dog revealed itself to *also* be a witch, ancient and powerful, and master of the witch cats. This was the Witch Dog! And it slew the family and used their body parts for potions to create more witch cats.

Metamorph
By
Kevin J. Kennedy

Best drug ever, they said. Nothing like it; first one is free. You know the drill... get you hooked, and they have you.

Metamorph they called it. It physically changed people. The more you took, the more you changed. What the fuck did I care? I had always been a junky, moving from one high to another, so I tried it.

They weren't lying, it's fantastical.

It happened quickly.

I began to morph into something spider- like: extra limbs, webbing capabilities, the lot.

My hunger's grown, and I imagine what the dealers will taste like as my children begin hatching

Sustenance
By
Rebecca Brae

Deep powder tempted me off the ski run. I hit a root under the snow and fell into a tree well. The walls will collapse if I move. I don't want to suffocate. Hopefully Mark finds my trail.

So cold. Can't move. Is a branch under my jacket?

It pierces between my ribs. Wriggles deeper.

The tree takes everything. Icy sap creeps through my veins. My heart no longer beats, yet I live.

Mark finds me. Digs.

I thought the tree was moving but it's us, together. Mark struggles, screams. His spine snaps like a twig. His warmth sustains us.

It's a Twin Thing
By
Tom Deady

I watched the crazies from the waiting room. Some stared vacantly, others just grinned, their lips moving in conversations with themselves. My favorites were the ones that flailed around like spastic air traffic controllers. I wondered which flavor my twin brother was. I hadn't seen him since he'd murdered our father, bludgeoning him with a hammer until there was nothing left of his skull but a soupy mix of brains and shattered bone. I giggled a little at this. Now, Mom spends all her time visiting him. I wondered what it would feel like to use the hammer on her.

Static Nightmare
By
Sarah Tantlinger

Darkness swallows me and I am overly aware – a hypnagogic soul, pliant for paralysis. Cannot move, cannot speak. Eyes open, rapidly swishing left, right, up, down, desperate to find reality. The sandman floats above, mouth in a cold line as he shoves coarse, golden grains into my sockets, scratching the irises and rubbing pain into lethargic nerves. Relax, he whispers. Relax, my brain answers the demon who traipses around my sheets, dusting his sooty prints like a halo around my pillow. No angel rescues me. Only darkness. Only the pleading scream inside my head as sand chokes down all movement.

Jack
By
Valerie Lioudis

As my life slipped away, I looked around the empty room. It was absent of others, and even things. Nothing would be left behind in this world other than my body, and once found, it would be stashed under the dirt to rot away out of sight. My entire existence would be erased when I took my last breath and none alive would mourn the loss. Instead they would spend generations trying to find me through my work. I left the clues behind for them to solve in the victims and locations I picked. I wonder... will my masterpiece work?

Trapped
By
David Owain Hughes

Sally awoke to the ground shaking.

"What happened, and why am I on the floor?" She stood as the earth tremors ended. Snow fell. "Why am I outside? I remember cleaning Jessica's bedroom..."

Fear clutched her when she realised her surroundings were fake.

"No, it can't be!"

Sally fled the wannabe city and slammed into a glass wall, her horrors realised. Beyond the barrier Sally saw her daughter, Jessica, replacing her snow globe on her shelf.

"Jessie, help – I'm trapped!" Sally slammed her fists against the glass but it was no good. Nobody would hear, or see, from Sally again...

Feed the Crop
By
Mark Cassell

I give up yelling into the gloom and no longer struggle against my bonds. The stink of damp wood and rotten vegetables clogs my senses.

Finally, the boy speaks.

"When people begin to ask questions, that's when I put them in the crop."

He touches the warm vegetation that coats my body, fingers probing the many lacerations across my chest ... and removes something. It squelches. There's little pain, only relief. He lifts the filth to his mouth.

"The crop needs to be fed." He bites into it, and chews. "As do I."

I wish I had never asked questions.

The Wishing Well
By
RJ Roles

Kevin waited as his classmates completed their work. He'd been waiting patiently all week for this. The first had been Jimmy, a constant bully. He'd tricked him into going to the well, telling him a girl was waiting to give him a kiss. Stupid. The stone crushed his skull. His body never made a sound after Kevin dumped it inside. That night, his parents bought him the bike he'd been wanting— a wish come true! He eyed Lisa. She'll never laugh at him again. The bell rang. He smiled. "Lisa, I have something to show you." He wanted that Gameboy

Fire
By
Joe X. Young

Sarah prodded the fire with a stick, molten plastic from Wayne's PlayStation stuck to the end. She emptied the last of his games from a holdall onto the bonfire. Tears striped her smoke- speckled cheeks; she stood back from the searing heat, not wishing to inhale anything that may harm their baby. Sarah was sick of the arguments, of course; Wayne didn't want children, he was a big kid himself. Accidents happen. She took off her wedding ring, threw that on the bonfire, his life in flames. By morning, she too would be gone, leaving his bones cooling in ashes.

Of Bubbles and Illusions
By
H.R. Boldwood

Trixie, the bubble dancer at The Palace, was Ozzie's favorite mistake. More than once he drowned his trouble in double shots and paid the pretty blonde for a tumble in his tiny twin bed. There, sharing long-forgotten dreams, they escaped a world determined to spin without them. She'd leave his loft at daybreak, taking with her the only sun he'd ever known.

In time, Trixie's opaque bubbles and feathered fans gave way to younger, artless sirens who left nothing to the imagination. But Ozzie held on tight. He knew Trixie's bubble gave life meaning. Everything else was just illusion.

How to Disappear in the Big City
By
Adriaan Brae

Warm water alerts the swarm to a victim above.

Young ones rush to the source, slim enough to slither through the drain holes. Head back under the stream, eyes shut, the prey never feels the stingers. Paralysis comes quickly. Razor sharp mandibles gouge and tear at any flesh they can reach.

Throat frozen, leaning rigid against cold tile, the prey wheezes desperately for rescue that will never come. It takes hours to carve the body into pieces small enough to wash through the grate. The swarm is sated.

Next week the tiny apartment is rented again.

Cash only.

No questions.

The Curious Case of Shadow Man
By
David Owain Hughes

They say he roams the streets, alleys and roads at night, and that he can be seen skulking around graveyards, homes and the like – peeping in windows for people to snatch.

Children are his favourite, but an elitist he is not.

He gobbles up his prey in shadow puppets, cast off floors and walls like traps, before dropping them in his bag and taking them to his depths. Never to be seen again.

Their bones have built his palaces; their eyes have studded his crowns.

Is he a ghost, or is he man?

Nobody knows, for he dwells in darkness…

One Witch's Cure for Vandalism
By
Sarina Dorie

"Why are you licking my windows?" the wicked witch asked the child.

She didn't look like the kind of witch who owned a gingerbread cottage in the woods. She was tall, slender, and young.

"To see if they taste good." The child crunched down on white icing. "Just so you know, your fence is stale."

"It's not stale. It's made from rice flour."

"Yuck! I wouldn't have eaten it if I had known."

The witch hammered a sign onto the gate with the words:

This home is healthy… Gluten-free. Low-fat. Low sugar. No corn syrup.

She had no more incidents.

No Breath to Scream
By
Robert W. Easton

Jacob felt his gut churn in hunger. The clothing donation bin beckoned; the shelter paid a dollar a pound for used clothes.

He opened the drawer. It was angled like a mailbox. The gleam of black garbage bags was within reach, provided he entered part way.

Scrambling up, he slid face first, wriggling his chest against the hard metal edge. Breathing became impossible, though he could get the weight off further in. Suddenly he realized, 'Oh God, I'm stuck!'

The garbage bags began moving. Helpless, Jacob watched rats boil and snarl upwards, clawing and biting. No breath to even scream.

Fur and Teeth
By
Rebecca Brae

Can't run. Can't hide. I'm lying in a sleeping bag, inside a zippered tent.

Bestial huffing drowns out my husband's snoring. A massive shadow paces around us, silhouetted between the orange nylon and rising sun. Its swampy musk invades my senses and kills all logic.

The tent shudders as a thick tongue rasps against the fabric inches from my face, tasting.

Sam snorts in his sleep. A chaos of orange and red, fur and teeth, erupts. Pain. I escape through a tear, slick with blood, and jerk to a stop. Screaming, I'm dragged back by a tether of my intestines.

No One Believes
By
Jay Sigler

A long, bony finger taps on the glass wall that is one wall of my new home. Giant black eyes set deep inside an elongated skull peer in at me with curiosity. Days ago, I pounded the glass, yelling to be returned. Today, I know this is my new reality. Resistance was futile.

No one believed me when I spoke about the light shining from the center of my cornfield. No one believed me when I spoke about the weird humming that had become a constant at the farmhouse. I barely believed it myself. But I do now.

Tap. Tap.

The Wolf and the Girl in the Red Dress
By
Michael Bray

The girl in the red dress never sees me because we wolves are a stealthy breed.

The hunter killed me, but my spirit will have its vengeance.

The smell. Blood and sinew. I wish I could tell it better, but I'm just a wolf, and don't have much of a way with words.

It is done and her blood soaks the earth.

She was as sweet as the grandmother was sour. My revenge is complete, yet I long to see her again. Is this my punishment? Am I destined to roam this godforsaken place in solitude?

What have I done?

Bedeviled
By
Mark Lukens

After years of searching, they had finally captured and killed the Devil, his dismembered pieces strewn across the holy ground of the ancient cemetery. A stormy sky raged above and the wind blew weeds and grasses among the tilted tombstones.

"Look!"

Peter saw it; one of the pieces of the Devil—a hand—was crawling towards an open grave. Peter tried to grab the hand, but he fell into the grave, slipping down into a tunnel that corkscrewed deep down into the bowels of the earth.

At the bottom Peter saw the Devil in front of him, whole again, laughing.

The Man Who Comes Around
By
Billy Chizmar

"The rhythm of thunder cannot mask his footsteps. Look! Through the floorboards, I can see his list. Its golden letters shimmer in the lightning sparks and I know that my name must be scrawled in his leather journal. Hear the tap-tap-tapping of his crooked pen against my bedroom door, I shall run while he's preoccupied there."

The Man was about to trudge to the bedroom belonging to his mark, when, by the same happenstance that anything slips, he dropped his ledger. An unfortunate bounce, and through the wooden floor it goes. Ah, what shame, to the basement he must go.

Victim
By
David Moody

I told them everything he did to me. I told them where and when and how hard. I told them what he said and how he forced me. I told them about the touching. The threats. I told his wife and kids. I told the papers. I told his boss. I posted everywhere that I could online. I showed everyone the scars and they all saw the tears. I told the police and they listened. Everybody knows about him now. I made it all up, but shit sticks. I just don't like the guy… wouldn't take no for an answer.

Walkers
By
James Newman

You know those "mall walkers" who spend their golden years doing stiff-legged laps past the Old Navy and the Cinnabon like they're on some sort of mission?

"They creep me out," a friend once joked. "Something in their eyes, if you cut them off."

My pal and his imagination, I thought at the time.

Until I looked closer . . .

I recognized in the faces of that silver-haired assemblage those who had gone missing in my city through the years.

Lollygaggers. Window-shoppers. Anyone who *got in their way*...

They're doomed to walk now, too.

Forever.

The Perfect Guests
By
Howard Carlyle

This wasn't a normal dinner party, the table was set to accommodate six people—me and my five guests. Each one of them had an enormous amount of time spent on them to make them look somewhat 'life-like', as they were a week ago. Flies have started to infest the place, but the guests haven't complained... I don't mind, either. What bothers me most is the smell coming from their decomposing corpses.

Dinner is served: steak cooked rare, creamy mashed potatoes, al dente vegetables... food fit to be served in any high class restaurant. I have the perfect guests.

Leftovers
By
Christina Bergling

Its large jaws are always coated, dripping in blood from the moment it decided not to press its sharp teeth into my flesh to this moment now, as I watch it devour another victim. The prey come in to the pit frequently— when she is done with them. The beast devours her discarded leftovers, all the way down to bones licked clean.

Yet not me. The beast refuses to eat me. After it has fed, lazy and fat, it crawls to me. Rumbling, it curls up at my side and places its massive sanguinary head on my thigh to sleep.

Night Visitor?
By
John Dover

The scrape and squeal of steel across glass irritated my eardrum. I sat up in bed to stare through the dark, nervous sweat permeating all my clothes and my breath fighting the silence of the room for dominance. The sharp shadows of furniture and discarded piles of laundry mocked my paranoia. It must have been the wind. A branch blown against the window. I wiped my hand across my damp forehead and lay back down. My breathing calmed and my eyelids grew heavy again, and then the cold, sharp finger of fear brushed across my terrorized soul and I screamed.

The Trolley
By
James Matthew Byers

Beneath the tarp, below the stench
Of rotting corpses' flesh,
The souls of children fed the wench
Who lured them in her mesh.
The innocence of gut and glam
Became her humble pie.
She chomped away on human lamb
And feasted on each cry.
The wheels would creak and scrape and groan
Amid the pressing weight.
"A hundred bodies," she would moan,
"I led them to their fate!"
And Agnes Gallow cast a spell
Upon her soulless shape
The while she summoned things from Hell
Allowing their escape.
An eerie glow,
A tragic folly.
Witches know
What's in the trolley.

Preserving Jar
By
Lee Murray

Shaking, I pat the floor. A newspaper, some tins, a rubber band.

The band crumbles—useless.

In the dark, I check the timber treads. A shelf… and a preserving jar! I unscrew the lid. Sniff. Pears. I'm suspicious. Does he know about the jar?

There are always consequences.

Fighting doubt, I dash the bottle against the risers. It shatters, gushing juice and fruit. I hold my breath, expecting the door, the light, him…

Nothing…

I pluck the shard from a crack, test it on my palm, then hide it in my pocket.

I'm still shaking when he unlocks the door.

The Hunter
By
James McCulloch

He watched from afar as the group of young alpha males whooped and hollered at the passing girls. The hatred and bile inside him growing with every insult thrown. By the time one of them split from the pack, he felt sick to his stomach.

Alone, the boy walked home through the woods, unaware of his surroundings— the glare and music from his phone drowning out the world.

The hunter grabbed him by the mouth, slipping his knife between the boy's fourth and fifth rib, kissing him on the nape as he removed the blade.

It was all too easy.

Doomed
By
Feind Gottes

We only did as we were told. We gathered our supplies and got ourselves underground. It was the only safe place from the horrors roaming the surface. They never told us how long it would last.

The darkness came first. Our batteries ran out after six months. Another three, even with severe rationing, and our food was gone. Venturing out for supplies meant certain death, so was impossible. The old oak had fallen against our only exit— Hercules couldn't move it.

Desperate times led to desperate, horrific acts. Sacrifices had to be made.

We only did as we were told.

Laid to Rest
By
Derek Shupert

David lay bound and gagged in the cavernous dirt grave. His legs and arms were restrained, mouth sealed shut with tape. His pleas were nothing more than a muffled scream that was barely audible. His eyes strained to pierce the veil of darkness that surrounded him.

Hovering above him to his right, the ghastly silhouette of a man draped all in black stood hunched over. The sound of earth being shuffled about caught his attention, followed by something wet and clumpy hitting his face. It took David a few moments to realize what was happening—he was being buried alive.

An Eye for a Tooth
By
Mike Duke

Matt sat on the playground, spitting blood and a broken tooth onto Tommy Biggins' shoes.

"Ooooh fuck!" exclaimed Randy Powelson. "He got blood on your brand-new Nike's, Tom! Fuck him up, man!"

Tommy roared; punted the smaller boy in the side. Ribs fractured.

Matt wheezed, struggled to stand - eyes burning with malice, neck stiff, face like flint. His whole body shook with adrenaline and hate.

"C'mon, Tommy." Sarcasm dripped from Matt's bloody tongue. "Bet you can't do that again."

Tommy's fist lashed out but the boxcutter Matt held glinted, struck first. Tommy clutched at his bleeding eye, pinwheeling, screaming.

Afterword

So, you have reached the end of our second drabble book. I hope it was a fun ride. I'm sure throughout the book you have discovered a whole host of authors that are new to you. I'd encourage you to check out their author pages on Amazon or Goodreads. There are no author bios in this book as they would be longer than the drabbles but all can be easily found online.

Thanks for picking up the book. If you have time, leave us a review somewhere as it helps others find the book.

Kev

Printed in Great Britain
by Amazon